CALL OF
THE WILD

ORIGINAL BY JACK LONDON

RETOLD BY PAULINE FRANCIS

Evans   **Marshall Cavendish**
Education

Published by Evans Brothers Limited
2A Portman Mansions
Chiltern Street
London W1U 6NR
United Kingdom

This edition published in collaboration with
Marshall Cavendish Education, 2007
© Evans Brothers Limited, 2005

Printed in China

British Library Cataloguing in Publication data
Francis, Pauline
    Call of the Wild. - (Fast Track Classics)
    1. Wolves 2. Children's stories
    I. Title II. London, Jack, 1876-1916
    823.9'14 [J]

ISBN: 0237533170
13-digit ISBN: 9780237533175

For related activities go to:
www.fasttrackclassics.com

www.evansbooks.co.uk
www.mcelt.co.uk

CALL OF THE WILD

CANCELLED

Introduction

Jack London was born in 1876, in the American State of Pennsylvania. At the age of fifteen, he left home to travel around North America. He lived the life of a tramp and spent many hours reading in local libraries. Then he decided to study at the University of California.

Jack left university because he was caught up in the excitement of the gold rush in the 1890s. Gold had been discovered in the River Klondike, in the Yukon Territory of Northwest Canada. Thirty thousand people travelled to this area, hoping to make their fortune. Dawson was the town that grew up around the gold hunters and it is still the main town of this region.

During the gold rush, many of these people travelled from the south (London calls it the 'Southland') to the Alaskan border (London calls it the 'Northland') for the first time. They were not used to the cold weather and many died on the way. In the long winter months, transport was only possible on sledges, pulled by dogs called huskies. There was a shortage of large, strong dogs. Dog-dealers stole dogs from the south and sold them to the frozen north. Buck, the hero of this book, was one of them.

Unfortunately, Jack London came back from the Klondike with no gold at all. But it was there that he had an idea for this story – *The Call of the Wild*. It was published in 1903 and became a huge bestseller. This book was followed in 1906 by another popular dog story called *White Fang*.

By 1913, Jack London was one of the most highly-paid and widely read writers in the world. Unfortunately, he drank too much, and wasted a great deal of his money. In 1916, when he was forty years old, Jack London killed himself.

CHAPTER ONE

Kidnap in California

Buck could not read the newspapers, or he would have known that trouble was brewing. Not just for him, but for all strong, long-haired dogs along the Californian coast. And why? All because men, searching in the Arctic darkness, had found gold. Thousands of men were rushing into the Northland. These men wanted dogs to pull their sledges, and the dogs they wanted had to be heavy, with strong muscles and furry coats to protect them from the frost.

But Buck knew nothing about this. He lived at a big house in the sun-kissed Santa Clara Valley, in California. Judge Miller's place, it was called. The whole place was his. He dived into the swimming tank; he went hunting with the Judge's sons; he looked after the Judge's daughters on their walks; he carried the Judge's grandsons on his back and on winter nights, he lay at the Judge's feet before the roaring fire.

Buck had ruled this kingdom for four years. Buck's father was a St. Bernard dog; but Buck was not quite as heavy – only a hundred and forty pounds, because his mother was a small shepherd dog. He liked hunting and this had hardened his muscles. He could have been

mistaken for a gigantic wolf, except for the splash of
white hair on his chest and brown flecks on his nose and
above his eyes.

So this was Buck in the autumn of 1897, when the
gold rush to the Klondike was at its peak. But Buck did
not know about the gold, and he did not know that
Manuel, one of the gardeners, needed money. One day,
Manuel took Buck for a walk through the orchard and
down to the railway station. There he put a rope around

Buck's neck, under his collar.

"Twist it, an' you'll choke 'im," Manuel told the stranger at the station.

Buck accepted the rope because he had learned to trust in the men he knew. But when the rope was put in the stranger's hands, he growled with anger. To his surprise, the rope tightened around his neck. Buck could hardly breathe. He jumped at the stranger angrily; but he grabbed Buck by the throat and flung him over his back. The rope tightened again. Buck hung there unconscious.

When he opened his eyes again, Buck was on a train. He sprang angrily towards the man sitting next to him. He took Buck by the throat and squeezed the breath out of him. Half-conscious, Buck felt the man taking off his dog collar and the rope. Then he was flung into a wooden cage.

Several times during the journey, whenever a door opened, Buck jumped to his feet, expecting the Judge or his sons to fetch him. But they never came. The journey was long. Buck was put onto a waggon, a truck, a ferry steamer, and an express train where he did not eat or drink for two nights. He had never been so badly treated in his life. The shock of it brought on a fever, and his throat and tongue became dry and swollen. His eyes were bloodshot. Buck looked like an angry monster.

The Judge would not have recognised him now.

CHAPTER TWO

The man in the red sweater

The express train pulled into the town of Seattle. Buck was taken to a small yard where a man in a red sweater came to look at him.

"Here comes my next tormentor," thought Buck. He hurled himself against the bars of the cage. The man smiled grimly and fetched a hatchet and a wooden club.

The man hit the cage with the hatchet. Buck rushed at the splintering wood and sank his teeth into it. Wherever the hatchet fell, there was Buck, snarling and growling.

"Now you red-eyed devil," said the man, when he had made an opening wide enough for Buck. He dropped his hatchet and picked up the wooden club.

Buck got ready to spring. His hair bristled, his mouth foamed, his mad, red eyes glittered. He threw himself straight at the man and opened his jaws in mid-air, ready to bite him. Suddenly, his jaw closed sharply and he fell to the ground, stunned.

The man had hit him with his club.

Buck got quickly to his feet. He jumped at the man, barking loudly. The man hit him again. Buck jumped more than twelve times, and each time, the man knocked him to the ground.

After the last blow, Buck staggered around the yard. Blood flowed from his mouth and nose. His beautiful long hair was flecked with bloody saliva. He was too tired to jump again. But this did not stop the man. He came towards Buck, raised the club high and struck Buck's nose. The pain was so terrible that Buck leaped into the air. The man caught him with his hand and threw him down and struck him again.

Buck lost consciousness.

A little later, he opened his eyes and watched the man in the red sweater. He knelt down and patted Buck's head and gave him a drink of water, and then chunks of red meat.

"Well, Buck, my boy," he said, "we've had our little fight. The best thing we can do is let it go at that. You've learned your place, and I know mine. Be a good dog, and all will go well. Be a bad dog and I'll knock the stuffin' outa you. Understand?"

"I'm beaten," thought Buck, "but I'm not broken. I don't stand a chance against this man."

Buck never forgot the lesson he learned that day. It was the first time he had come across this simple law – a man with a club was a master to be obeyed.

A few weeks later, a small man came to the yard. He did not speak English well. His eyes lit up when he saw Buck.

"Dat dog is one in a thousand, eh? How much?" he asked.

"Three hundred, and a present at that, Perrault," the dog-dealer replied.

Perrault bought Buck, and another dog called Curly. He took them straight to a steamship, where they joined two more dogs, Spitz and Dave. A tall man called François, a French-Canadian like Perrault, looked after all the dogs. Both men were kind, calm and fair in their treatment. Buck had never met men like these before. He grew to respect them, although never to love them.

Outside, the weather grew colder and colder. One day, François took the dogs up on deck. At his first step upon the cold surface, Buck's feet sank into a white, mushy something, very much like mud. More of this white stuff was falling through the air.

Buck shook himself, but more of it fell on him. He sniffed it curiously, then licked it. It felt as hot as fire for a moment, then it melted away. The men on deck laughed as Buck played with the first snow he had ever seen.

But when the steamship sailed into port, the nightmare began for Buck.

CHAPTER THREE

Northland

Every hour of Buck's first day in Northland was filled with shock and surprise. There was no safety, no sun, no rest. Every moment, his life was in danger. Buck had to be alert all the time. The dogs and men here were all savages. He learned a terrible lesson that first day. And Curly was the victim.

Curly, a friendly animal, had walked over to a husky dog just outside Perrault's camp. There was no warning of what was going to happen. Buck watched in horror. He saw a flash of teeth, a swift leap, and Curly's face split open from eye to jaw. Within seconds, thirty or forty huskies ran to watch the fight. They stood licking their lips.

Curly ran towards the husky again. In a second, he knocked her down. The other huskies had been waiting for this moment. They came closer, snarling and yelping. Soon, poor Curly was buried, screaming, under them. In less than two minutes, she was limp and lifeless and torn to pieces in the snow.

"So that is how life is here," thought Buck, "no fair play. Once down and that's the end of you. Well, I'll *never* go down."

There was another shock for Buck later that day. François put a leather harness around him and fastened him to a sledge.

"So I am to be a working dog," thought Buck, "just like the horses were at Judge Miller's!"

But now Buck was too wise to rebel and he did his best.

Perrault came back to the camp with more new dogs. Now he had nine dogs in the team to pull his sledge. In the morning, they would set off for the town of Dawson, delivering letters and messages for the Canadian Government.

The night brought new dangers for Buck. Perrault and François had pitched their tent and it glowed with yellow candlelight in the snow. Buck crawled inside to sleep with them. But the men shouted at him, and threw a saucepan at his head until he ran out into the cold.

Buck lay on the snow and tried to sleep. The wind was icy and the frost made him stand up again. He wandered around sadly, snarling at every wild dog that came near. How was he going to survive this terrible night?

Suddenly, Buck had an idea.

"I'll find out where my team-mates are sleeping," he thought.

Buck set off through the camp. Where were they all? They had disappeared! Buck shivered violently and his tail drooped. Suddenly, the snow gave way under his front legs and he began to sink. Something wriggled under him. He sprang back, snarling. A dog yelped. Buck went back to the spot and looked down. There in the snow, in a snug ball, lay one of the new dogs. Another lesson! So that was the way they did it, eh? Buck dug a hole for himself. The heat from his body filled the space and he fell asleep.

"That Buck for sure learn quick," François called to Perrault.

"I am glad of it," nodded Perrault, "I must have good dogs to get us to Dawson on time."

They set off that morning. Although the work was hard, Buck was amazed how much the dogs changed when they were working together. They became alert and anxious that the work would go well. Buck was harnessed in front of a dog called Dave, and behind Sol-leks, a lean old dog with one eye. These two dogs were his teachers, nipping him with their teeth whenever he made a mistake. The rest of the team was in front, in single file, led by Spitz.

It was a hard run across glaciers, through deep snow drifts, over great mountains and along a chain of lakes. Perrault was in a hurry. But he always took care of his dogs. He knew the ice well and never took them where it was too thin.

Day after day, they travelled across the Arctic. The men always pitched camp in the dark. Then the dogs ate their pound and a half of dried salmon, and crawled to sleep in the snow. Buck was always hungry. He learned to eat quickly, forgetting the dainty manners of his old life. He even stole food. He was learning how to survive.

Buck changed because he had no choice, not because he wanted to change. His muscles became as hard as iron. He no longer felt pain. He could eat anything, however disgusting. His scent and sight became sharper. He could smell the wind so well that he knew where to dig his shelter at night. His hearing became so good that he could hear the faintest sound even in his sleep.

Buck slowly became wilder, like dogs used to be. He discovered dog ways long forgotten after years of living in houses. Sometimes, on still cold nights, he pointed his nose at a star and howled like a wolf. The wild beast in Buck was strong, and it grew and grew in his new, harsh life.

And soon he wanted to dominate the other dogs – especially Spitz.

CHAPTER FOUR

Buck makes an enemy

Spitz soon sensed the change in Buck. He went out of his way to bully him, to start a fight. And that fight, Spitz knew, would end in the death of one of them.

One night, early in the trip, Spitz put Buck to the test. They camped on the shore of a lake. The wind cut like a knife, and blew the snow against them. Buck made his nest under a rock. When he left to fetch his fish, Spitz wriggled into it. This was too much for Buck. The beast in him roared. He sprang on Spitz with an anger that surprised them both.

"Teach 'im a lesson, Buck" called François, "the dirty thief!"

The dogs circled each other, both willing to fight.

Suddenly, in the distance, Perrault shouted. Then they heard the sound of his club on a bony body, followed by a yelp of pain. At that moment, the camp was alive with starving wild husky dogs – eighty or a hundred of them. They had crept in during the fight, crazed by the smell of food.

Buck had never seen such dogs. They were skeletons with blazing eyes and fangs. They were mad with hunger. They pushed the team-dogs back against the rocks. Three huskies sprang onto Buck and ripped his head and shoulders. Buck caught one by the throat and was sprayed with blood. The taste of the blood made him fiercer, and he attacked another husky.

Suddenly, Buck felt teeth sink into his throat. It was Spitz. Buck guessed his plan. If Buck fell to the ground, the huskies would kill him. He remembered Curly's death.

"I'll *never* go down," he thought.

Buck did not fall. He threw off Spitz and ran after the others onto the lake. The team was a sorry sight. Every dog was wounded in several places. Half their food had been eaten. The huskies had even chewed through the leather straps of the harness. Perrault was worried.

"We still have four hundred miles to travel," he said. "Let's hope none of them have caught rabies from those wild dogs." The next part of the trail, across the Thirty Mile River, was the hardest yet. The water was so wild that the ice was very thin in places. The temperature dropped to fifty degrees below zero. Perrault led them on for six terrible days, from dawn to dusk.

Buck's feet were not as hard as the feet of the other huskies. All day he limped in great pain and lay down like a dead dog when they set up camp. He could not even fetch his fish and François had to bring it over to him. François even rubbed Buck's feet and cut off the

top of his own moccasins to make four shoes for him. One morning, François forgot to bring the moccasins to Buck. Buck lay on his back, his feet in the air until François fetched them. This made Perrault's face twist itself into a grin for the first time in weeks!

One morning, one of the dogs, called Dolly, gave a terrible howl. It was long and high and made the other dogs tremble with fear. Then she sprang at Buck. He had never seen a dog go mad with rabies. He knew that here was horror and he ran away from it. Dolly ran after him, frothing at the mouth. All the time, he could hear her snarling, just one leap behind him. Buck turned back through the wood, towards François who was now holding his axe high. Buck ran under it, then it crashed down on mad Dolly's head.

Buck staggered over to the sledge and panted for breath.

Spitz saw his chance again. He sank his teeth into Buck. But François saw what was happening and whipped Spitz until he ran away.

"He is a devil, dat Spitz," said Perrault.

"Listen," said François, "some fine day, Buck get mad an' chew Spitz all up, an' spit heem out on de snow. I know."

From then on, it was war between Buck and Spitz. Buck amazed Spitz. All the other dogs from the South were soft and died exhausted by the work and the cold. Buck was different. *He* was as cunning and as strong as the huskies. *He* was now one of the trail dogs and he was proud of it.

The fight did not break out until they were on the return journey from Dawson. By now, the dogs were restless. Buck was quietly turning them against Spitz. They no longer feared him. They no longer worked as one dog in the harness.

One night, after supper, one of the dogs sprang on a rabbit and missed. In a second, the whole team ran after it, joined by fifty huskies from a nearby camp. The thirst for blood and the joy of the kill were strong in Buck that night. He ran at the head of the pack. He wanted to kill that wild animal with his teeth. He wanted to wash his nose in its warm blood.

Buck felt truly alive at that moment. He felt his true dog-nature.

When he came round the next bend, he saw a larger frosty shape leap from the overhanging bank into the path of the rabbit. It was Spitz. He broke the rabbit's back with his teeth and the dogs cried out in delight.

Buck did not cry out with them. He could not stop now. He pushed Spitz to the ground. They rolled over and over in the powdery snow. In a flash Buck knew it. The time had come. It was a fight to the death.

CHAPTER FIVE

Fight to the death

Spitz was used to fighting, and used to winning. But he never forgot that his enemy had the same desire to destroy him.

Over and over again, Buck tried to sink his teeth into the neck of the big white dog. They always met the teeth of the other dog. Then Buck rushed at Spitz, pretending to go for his throat. At the last minute, he drew back his head and rammed Spitz with his shoulder. But each time, Spitz leapt away. By now, Buck was streaming with blood and panting hard.

The fight was growing desperate.

And all this time, a circle of about sixty dogs watched them. Once, Buck fell over and they started to move forward. Buck stood up, almost before he touched the ground, and they sat down again to wait.

Buck had one great quality – imagination. He rushed towards Spitz' shoulder once more. At the last moment, he dipped low in the snow and closed his teeth around his enemy's front leg. There was a crunch of breaking bone.

Now the white dog faced Buck on three legs. Buck repeated his trick and broke the dog's right front leg.

Spitz struggled madly to stand up. He saw the silent circle of dogs, their eyes gleaming, their tongues hanging and their silvery breath drifting upwards. He had seen many circles like this one close in and kill a dog. It was his turn.

There was no hope for Spitz. Buck made his final run. The circle of dogs was so close that Buck could feel their breath on his back. They stood as still as stone. Only Spitz moved, snarling. The dogs suddenly moved forward and Spitz disappeared under them.

Buck stood and looked on, the successful champion who had made his kill and found it good.

In the morning, François looked at Buck's wounds.

"An' now we make good time," he told Perrault. "No more Spitz, no more trouble, sure."

François brought in Sol-leks to lead the pack. Furious, Buck sprang upon Sol-leks, pushed him back and took his place. François was angry, too. He pushed Buck away and brought back Sol-leks. The angry dog-driver picked up his club. Buck, remembering the man in the red sweater, slunk away.

Buck refused to join his team. François and Perrault chased him for an hour or so. They threw clubs at him; but Buck stayed away.

"We're late!" groaned Perrault.

At last, François untied Sol-leks and harnessed Buck at the head of the team. He was a good leader. Soon, the team worked together again, running as one dog.

Perrault was delighted. They made the run in record time. They averaged forty miles a day for two weeks. It was not too cold, and there was no new snow. It was their last ride together. Perrault and François took up new jobs and sold the dogs to the owners of the mail train. Now they had to make the run north to Dawson many times, taking letters to the men still searching for gold. Buck did not like it, but he still took a pride in his work.

When darkness fell, Buck loved to lie near the camp fire and stare dreamily into the flames. Sometimes, he thought of Judge Miller's big house in sun-kissed California, of the cement swimming tank. But more often he thought of the man in the red sweater, the death of Curly, and the great fight with Spitz. Buck was not homesick. These memories had no power over him. Far stronger were his dog-feelings. They were becoming fiercer every day.

In less than five months, the team had travelled twenty-five hundred miles. All the dogs were tired – so tired that at last, fresh dogs took their place.

That was how Buck came to be sold for the third time. And for the first time in his life, he did not trust his owners.

CHAPTER SIX

Disaster on the lake

His new owners were two men and a woman. The men called each other "Hal" and "Charles." The woman, Mercedes, was Charles' wife and Hal's sister. Charles was a middle-aged man with weak and watery eyes. His moustache hid his drooping lips. Hal was much younger, only nineteen or twenty. He wore a belt which carried his revolver and a hunting knife. Both men were out of place – and Buck's heart sank whenever he saw them.

A nice family party, going out to hunt gold!

As Hal and Charles began to load their sledge, the men from the next tent strolled over to watch them.

"It seems a bit top heavy," said one.

Charles ignored him and harnessed the dogs to the sledge. They pulled; but the sledge did not move.

"The lazy brutes, I'll show them!" shouted Hal. He picked up his whip.

"Oh, Hal, you musn't," cried Mercedes, snatching the whip from her brother.

"Precious lot you know about dogs," Hal sneered. "They're lazy, I tell you. Ask any of these men."

"They're weak, if you want to know," said one of the men. "They need a rest."

Hal's whip fell upon the dogs. They tried to pull the sledge again; but it wouldn't move.

"I don't care what happens to you," said another man, "but for the dogs' sake, I want to tell you. The runners on the sledge are frozen to the ground."

Hal listened this time. He broke the ice on the runners and, at last, the sledge moved. The dogs rushed towards the main street. As they turned, the sledge leaned, spilling everything into the street.

"Half the load and twice the dogs, if you want to reach Dawson," someone shouted.

Mercedes cried as she unpacked some of her clothes. She cried so much that she left things behind that they would need on the dangerous journey ahead. Charles and Hal bought six more dogs. Buck looked at them with disgust. Didn't they know that a sledge cannot carry enough food for fourteen dogs?

They lost time almost straight away. Their owners were so lazy that sometimes they did not leave camp at all. The dog-food ran low. The dogs pulled weakly because they were tired. Hal, not understanding this, doubled their rations of food. When the men were busy, Mercedes stole fish and brought it to them.

Soon, the under-feeding began. The six new dogs died first. The family began to quarrel over everything. The Arctic lost its glamour, the thought of gold lost its romance. As they began to suffer, they made the dogs suffer too.

Buck staggered on at the head of his team. Life was a nightmare. He pulled when he could. When he could not, he fell to the ground. He got up when he was whipped. His glossy hair hung limp, sticky with blood. He was thin, every bone showing through his skin. But Buck could not be broken. The man in the red sweater had proved that.

One by one, the dogs began to die. Soon, there were only seven left, including Buck. They were staggering bags of bones. Whenever they stopped, they dropped to the ground in the harness as if they were already dead. And when the whip lashed their bones, they staggered to their feet.

One sunny spring day, just when the ice was beginning to melt, they came to John Thornton's camp at the mouth of a river.

"What's the trail like from here?" Charles asked him.

"The ice is melting fast," said John Thornton. "Best wait until winter. I wouldn't risk my life on that ice for all the gold in Alaska."

"All the same, we'll go on to Dawson," said Hal.

He raised his whip.

"Get up there, Buck! Hi! Get up there!" he yelled.

The team slowly got up. All except Buck. He quietly

lay where he had fallen. He had made up his mind not to get up. He felt that something terrible was going to happen. The blows of the whip did not hurt him much. He felt numb. His body seemed a long way away.

Suddenly, John Thornton jumped on Hal and pushed him to the ground.

"If you strike that dog again, I'll kill you," he cried. His voice trembled.

"It's my dog," said Hal.

He wiped the blood from his mouth.

"Get out of my way," he snarled, "I'm going to Dawson."

Hal pulled out his hunting-knife. Mercedes screamed. Thornton knocked the knife from Hal's hand. Then he picked it up and cut Buck's harness.

"He's too near dead to be of any use," said Hal, angrily. "Let's go."

A few minutes later, the sledge pulled away from the bank and down the river. Buck and Thornton watched them. Suddenly, the back end of the sledge dropped down. Mercedes screamed. A whole section of ice gave way and dogs and humans disappeared into the yawning hole.

John Thornton and Buck looked at each other.

"You poor devil," said John Thornton.

And Buck licked his hand.

CHAPTER SEVEN

For the love of a man

Buck rested. His wounds healed, his muscles thickened and he put on weight. John Thornton was healing too. On the way to Dawson last winter, he had caught frostbite in his feet. He still had a slight limp. Now he was waiting for his friends, Hans and Pete, to bring a raft downriver and take him to Dawson.

Thornton had two other dogs – a little Irish setter who licked Buck's wounds, and a huge black dog with laughing eyes. They were never jealous of Buck. They were as kind and friendly as their master.

John Thornton was the perfect owner. He sat and talked to his dogs. He often held Buck's head between his hands and pretended to scold him. Then to show his love, Buck caught Thornton's hand in his mouth and held it without biting. Buck went wild with happiness when Thornton touched him or spoke to him. He would lie hour after hour, looking at his master's face.

But Buck did not become soft as he had been in the Southland. He was still a dog of the wild. He fought other dogs from other camps. He showed no mercy, no fear. Fear led to death, he knew that. Kill or be killed. Eat or be eaten. That was the law, and Buck obeyed it.

As Buck sat by the fire, he thought of other dogs, half-wolves and wild wolves. Each time he dreamed of them, he wanted to be with them. They seemed to call him deep in the forest. He wanted to turn his back on the fire and run after them. But his love for John Thornton pulled him back to the fire again. Other men were not important.

When the ice had melted on the river, Thornton's friends came with a raft. The three men found work in the saw-mills, floating tree logs up the mill on the river. One day, Thornton was on the raft in the middle of the river. His friends were trying to steady the raft with ropes from the bank.

Buck stood watching on the bank. His eyes never left his master. Suddenly, Thornton's raft flipped over and he was carried downstream towards the rapids. Buck jumped into the water immediately. He swam to Thornton, who caught hold of his tail. Buck tried to swim towards the bank, but the current was too strong. Thornton knew that they could not reach the bank together. He let go of Buck.

"Go, Buck! Go!" he shouted.

Buck swam alone to the bank. The men tied a rope to his shoulders and he jumped back into the water. He tried to reach his master many times until he was half-drowned and the men had to pull him to the bank.

There, he could still hear the faint sound of Thornton's voice. Buck set off again and managed to reach his master. Thornton put his arms around Buck's shaggy neck, and, strangling, suffocating, they were pulled to the bank.

The next winter, in Dawson, Buck became famous for the second time that year. The men in the bar were boasting about the strength of their dogs.

"Mine can pull a load weighing five hundred pounds," said one.

"Mine can pull six hundred," said another.

"Mine can pull seven hundred," said a man called Matthewson.

"Pooh! pooh!" said John Thornton, before he could stop himself, "Buck can pull a thousand pounds." He hesitated. "And he can pull it for a hundred yards."

"Well," said Matthewson, "I've got a thousand dollars that says he can't do it."

He slammed a sack of gold dust onto the counter. John Thornton did not know what to say. He had no thousand dollars. Suddenly, he caught sight of an old friend in the crowd. Thornton did something he had never done before – he borrowed money. Other people in the bar began to place bets. Then they all went outside into the freezing cold.

Thornton groaned when he saw Matthewson's sledge.

It was packed with sacks of flour and had a team of ten dogs. How could Buck do the work of ten dogs? Matthewson unharnessed his team and put the harness on Buck. Thornton knelt by Buck's side and rested his cheek against Buck's cheek.

"Do it for the love of me, Buck," he whispered.

Then he stood up.

"*Now*, Buck," he called.

Thornton's order rang out like a pistol-shot. Buck threw himself forward, head forward and down, his great chest low to the ground. The sledge trembled, lurched and stopped as one of Buck's feet slipped. Then it lurched again, half an inch, an inch, two inches… it never stopped again. The sledge gained speed until it moved steadily along.

Men cheered and threw their hats into the air, and shook hands. But Thornton fell on his knees beside Buck, tears streaming down his cheeks, and scolded him gently.

CHAPTER EIGHT

Searching for gold

When Buck earned sixteen hundred dollars in five minutes for John Thornton, he made it possible for his master to go to look for gold. Not in the Klondike River, but further east, to look for a lost gold mine where the gold nuggets were bigger and better than any in the west. Many men had looked for it, few had found it and some had never returned from their journey.

The three men set off with their dogs. They sledged seventy miles up the Yukon valley and into the high mountains. Buck had never been happier, running and hunting in the wild. For weeks on end, they camped here and there. Sometimes, they all went hungry. At others, they ate too much. Summer came and they rafted across blue mountain lakes and unknown rivers.

The next winter, they came close to the lost mine; but the path suddenly ended. The following spring, they reached a wide river valley where gold shone like butter. The men looked no further. Each day they worked hard and stacked their gold in skin bags.

There was no work for the dogs to do. Day after day, Buck lay by the fire. More and more, he heard the call from the forest. He longed to be there. Once, he went into the forest, barking softly. He thrust his nose into the cool moss and the black soil. He crouched behind fallen trees, watching. Buck did not know why he did these things. But he could not stop himself.

Strange feelings ran through Buck. He would be lying in the camp, dozing in the sun, when suddenly his ears would prick up. He would listen for a while, then spring to his feet and run for hours. Sometimes, he lay in the grass and watched the birds for a whole day. He loved to run at dusk, always looking and listening for the call to go further.

One night, he suddenly woke up. His hair bristled. His nostrils sniffed the air. From the forest came a call. He heard it clearly this time – a long howl. He knew he had heard that sound before. He ran towards the cry. When it was very near, he slowed down. Carefully he moved forward to an open place among the trees. Buck stared in front of him.

Sitting in front of him, his nose pointed at the sky, was a wolf.

Buck half-crouched and half-walked forward. His tail was straight, his whole body ready to spring. The wolf ran away at the sight of him. Buck followed, and cornered the wolf in the bed of a stream. It turned to face Buck, snarling and snapping his teeth.

Buck did not attack the wolf. He circled around him

in a friendly way. Every time the wolf ran away, Buck caught him again. At last, the wolf gave in. It sniffed Buck's nose. Then they played together, until the wolf walked away. Buck followed him. They ran side by side in the twilight, through the night until the sun rose.

Buck was happy. He had answered the call. He had run with his wood brother at last. Then he remembered John Thornton.

John Thornton was eating dinner when Buck ran into the camp. He knocked his master over, licked his face and bit his hand.

"You old fool," said Thornton, holding Buck's head between his hands.

For two days, Buck never left the camp. He followed Thornton everywhere. Buck watched him eat and work and sleep. But after two days, the call came again. It was louder this time. Buck began to feel restless. He thought about his wild brother all the time. Soon, Buck ran back to the forest, but the wild wolf did not come.

Now Buck began to stay away from the camp for days at a time. He went beyond to the mountains at the head of the river where he had run before. Buck fished for salmon in a stream. He killed a big black bear and his longing for blood became stronger. He was a killer, he knew that.

The men in the camp noticed the change in Buck. He was at his peak – quick to respond to a sound, quick to defend or attack. His muscles were full of strength. He was full of life.

"There was never a dog like Buck," said John Thornton, as he watched Buck march out of the camp.

That was the last time he saw Buck.

CHAPTER NINE

Indian attack!

John Thornton did not see the other changes that took place when Buck reached the forest. He no longer marched. He became a dog of the wild, crawling on his belly like a snake and leaping to strike at small animals. He caught fish in the water pools, and beavers building their dams. He wanted to eat what he had killed.

One day, at the end of summer, Buck was returning to the camp. He ran gently, hour after hour, heading straight home through strange country. He sensed that something was different. The birds talked of it, the squirrels chattered about it and the very breeze whispered it. Several times, he stopped and sniffed the air. He sensed that something terrible was going to happen, or had happened already.

As Buck dropped into the valley towards the camp, he slowed down. Something was wrong.

Three miles away from the camp, Buck came across fresh footprints which led straight to the camp. The hair on Buck's back began to bristle. He hurried on. He noticed each thing that was different. The forest was completely silent. The birds had flown. The squirrels had run away.

Suddenly, Buck sniffed the air. He picked up a new scent and followed it to a clump of trees. Thornton's big black dog lay there, on his side, an arrow sticking through his body. He was dead. A hundred yards further on, Buck came upon one of the sledge dogs Thornton had bought in Dawson. This dog was dying; but Buck passed around him without stopping.

He could hear faint voices coming from the camp, rising and falling in a sing-song chant. Buck crept on his belly towards the camp clearing. On the way, he found Hans, lying on his face and feathered with arrows like a porcupine.

Buck peered through the trees, looking for the wooden hut. The hair on his neck and shoulders stood straight up. A terrible rage swept through him. The hut was burned to the ground and Yeehat Indians were dancing around it.

Buck did not even know that he was growling out aloud; but he did. For the first time in his life, Buck allowed his feelings to show. He forgot to be cunning, because of his great love for John Thornton. The Yeehats stopped dancing when they heard Buck's terrible roar. Buck sprang at the chief and ripped his throat open. He went on to the next man. He was never still, destroying and tearing. The Indians tried to shoot arrows at him, but they shot each other instead.

Then, terrified, they fled into the woods. Buck was truly the Devil that day. He ran after them. He dragged them down like deer as they raced through the trees. At last, he left them and went back to the camp and began his search for Pete – and John Thornton.

He found Pete, still wrapped in his blanket, killed as he slept. There were footprints close by and they showed a desperate struggle. Buck followed their scent to the edge of a deep pool. By the edge, head and front paws in the water, lay the faithful little Irish setter.

Buck followed the scent of his master into the pool. But he could find no scent out there. Then he saw it – the body of John Thornton.

CHAPTER TEN
The call of the wild

All day long, Buck stayed in the camp. He roamed about, restless. His master's death made him feel empty – a hunger that no food could fill. Sometimes, when he looked at the bodies of the Yeehats, he felt a great pride. He had killed a man – the biggest kill of all. He sniffed the bodies curiously. They had died so easily. It was harder to kill a husky than these men. From now on, he would not be afraid of them.

That night, a full moon rose over the trees. The land seemed as bright as day. Suddenly, with the coming of the night, Buck felt the forest come alive again. He stood up, listened and sniffed the air.

He heard a faint yelp, followed by other yelps. The yelps grew closer and louder. Buck walked to the centre of the open space and listened.

It was the call.

And never had Buck been more ready to obey it. John Thornton was dead. The last link to Man was broken.

A wolf pack had at last crossed the stream and come to hunt in Buck's valley. They poured into the clearing. Buck, as still as a statue, waited for them. The wolves were afraid at first because he was so still and large. Then the bravest wolf leaped straight at him. Like a flash, Buck struck and broke the wolf's neck. Then he stood, without moving, as before, as the wolf rolled in agony behind him.

Three other wolves ran at Buck. One after the other, they moved back, streaming blood from their throats or shoulders. Then the whole pack moved forward, eager to kill Buck. He stood high on his hind legs, snapping and slashing them. He was everywhere at once, swirling from side to side.

Buck moved back to the bank of the pool to stop the wolves getting behind him. He faced them and waited. He faced them so well that after half an hour, the pack moved back. Their tongues hung from their mouths and their teeth shone in the moonlight. Some lay down with their ears pricked. Others stood watching him. A few lapped water from the pool.

At last, an enormous grey wolf came towards Buck. It was his wolf brother. Buck had run with him for a night and a day. They touched noses.

Then an old wolf, covered in scars, came forward. Buck pulled back his lips in a snarl. But the wolf sniffed Buck's nose. Buck stopped snarling and sniffed the old wolf's nose. Buck waited.

The old wolf sat down, turned his pointed nose at the moon and howled his long wolf howl. The others sat down and howled. And now the call came to Buck. He, too, sat and howled.

Buck came out from the pool and the pack crowded around him, sniffing in a half-friendly, half-savage manner. The leaders of the pack ran into the woods. The wolves ran after them, yelping in chorus.

Buck watched them for a second. Then he ran, side by side with the wild brother, yelping as he ran.

At last, Buck had answered the call of the wild.

Some years later, the Yeehat Indians noticed
a change in the breed of the wolves. Some had splashes
of brown on their head and nose. Others had white
splashes on their chests.

The Yeehats tell many stories – of tribesmen found
with their throats ripped open… of footprints in the
snow bigger than any wolf's footprints… and of the
great dog that comes in the summer to the clearing in
the forest and howls by the river…

Glossary

Key:

adj	adjective
adv	adverb
n	noun
phr	phrase
phr v	phrasal verb
pl n	plural noun
vi	intransitive verb
vt	transitive verb

agony	*n*	great pain	46
alert	*adj*	very aware of what is happening	14
arrow	*n*	a long, thin piece of wood with a sharp metal point	42
belly	*n*	the stomach	41
bloodshot	*adj*	with red spots of blood	9
boast, to	*vi*	to say something in a proud way	35
breed	*n*	a particular type of an animal	48
brew: **trouble was brewing**	*phr*	a bad situation was developing	7
bristle, to	*vi*	if hair bristles, it stands on end	10
bully, to	*vt*	to frighten or hurt someone who is not as strong as you	19
caught: to be caught up	*phr v,* *passive*	if you are caught up in something, you are involved in it *(caught: past participle of **catch**)*	4
chant	*n*	a repetitive song	42
choke, to	*vt*	to stop someone breathing by holding their throat; to strangle	9

clearing	*n*	a small area without trees, in a wood or forest	42
club	*n*	a heavy piece of wood	10
clump	*n*	a group	42
corner, to	*vt*	if you corner an animal or a person, you force them into a place from which they can't escape	38
crazed	*adj*	mad	19
crouch, to	*vi*	to keep low to the ground	38
cunning	*adj*	clever and deceiving	23
curiously	*adv*	in an interested way	12
current	*n*	a flowing movement in a river	34
dainty	*adj*	delicate; feminine	18
dam	*n*	a wall built across a river that stops it flowing	41
dealer	*n*	a person who buys and sells something	4
dip, to	*vi*	to make a sudden downward movement	24
downstream	*adv*	down a river	34
doze, to	*vi*	to sleep gently	38
drift, to	*vi*	to float gently	25
drooping	*adj*	hanging loosely	28
fair play	*n*	behaviour and attitudes that show justice and sympathy to everyone	14
fang	*n*	a long tooth	19
feathered with arrows	*phr*	with arrows all over it	42
fever	*n*	an illness which gives you a high body temperature	9

flecked	*adj*	spotted; dotted	11
flip over, to	*phr*	to turn over suddenly	34
flung	*past simple of fling; vt*	threw	9
foam, to	*vi*	to be full of bubbles; to froth	10
footprint	*n*	the shape of a foot	41
frost	*n*	the white crystals of ice that cover things on cold winter days	7
frostbite	*n*	damage to flesh caused by severe cold	33
froth, to	*vi*	to be full of bubbles; to foam	22
give way, to	*phr v*	to collapse; to fall away	16
glacier	*n*	a large area of ice in the mountains	16
glamour	*n*	the quality of being attractive and exciting	29
gleam, to	*vi*	to shine gently	25
glitter, to	*vi*	to shine gently	10
half -conscious	*adj*	not fully aware of what is happening around you; fainting	9
harness	*n*	straps used to attach a horse to a cart, for example	15
hatchet	*n*	an axe	10
head (of a river)	*n*	where a river starts from	40
hind (legs)	*adj*	back legs	46
in single file	*phr*	in a line, one behind the other	16

knock the stuffing out of someone, to	*phr*	to be violent towards someone and to make life very difficult for them	11
lap, to	*vt*	to drink using your tongue	46
lash, to	*vt*	to hit hard	30
lean	*adj*	thin	16
limp	*adj*	hanging loosely	14
limp, to	*vi*	to walk unevenly, because you have a sore foot or leg	20
link	*n*	something that joins things	45
load, to	*vt*	to pile goods into a vehicle	28
long for, to	*vi*	to want very much	37
lurch, to	*vi*	to make a sudden, violent movement forward	36
moccasins	*pl n*	a kind of shoe	22
moss	*n*	a kind of small, soft plant	38
mushy	*adj*	very soft	12
nostrils	*pl n*	the holes in the end of your nose	38
numb	*adj*	without any feeling	31
one in a thousand	*phr*	exceptionally good	12
orchard	*n*	an area where fruit trees are grown	8
overhanging	*adj*	which sticks out above something	23
pack (of dogs)	*n*	a group	23
peak	*n*	when something is at its peak, it is at its highest or biggest stage	8

peer, to	*vi*	to look carefully	42
pitch (a tent), to	*vt*	to put a tent up	15
place bets, to	*phr*	to bet money, for example, so that if what you say will happen does happen, you win a lot of money; to gamble	35
porcupine	*n*	an animal that is covered with sharp spikes	42
precious lot	*phr*	not a lot at all	28
put someone to the test, to	*phr*	to do something in order to find out just how strong etc. someone is	19
rabies	*n*	a serious illness that makes people and animals go mad and die	20
raft	*n*	a kind of simple, small, flat boat	33
ram, to	*vt*	to bang hard into	24
rapids	*pl n*	a section of fast-flowing, dangerous water on a river	34
roam, to	*vi*	to wander	45
roaring (fire)	*adj*	that is burning well	7
run	*n*	a journey	26
runner	*n*	a long piece of metal or wood that helps a sledge to slide over snow or ice	29
saliva	*n*	the liquid that you have in your mouth	11
savage	*n*	a wild and violent creature	14
scar	*n*	a mark left on the skin by an injury	46
scent	*n*	the sense of smell	18
scent	*n*	a smell	44

scold, to	*vt*	to talk angrily to someone because they have done something wrong	33
shaggy	*adj*	with long hair	35
shepherd dog	*n*	a dog that works with sheep	7
show mercy, to	*n*	if you show mercy to someone, you decide not to hurt them or you forgive them	33
slam, to	*vt*	if you slam something somewhere, you put it there very heavily and noisily	35
slash, to	*vt*	to cut violently	46
sledge	*n*	a kind of small cart used for carrying things over snow or ice	4
snarl, to	*vi*	to make an angry, growling noise	10
sniff, to	*vt*	to smell	12
snug	*adj*	warm; cosy	16
splinter, to	*vi*	to break into lots of small, sharp pieces	10
sprang	*past simple of* **spring***; vi*	jumped suddenly	9
stagger, to	*vi*	to walk very unsteadily	11
steadily	*adv*	at a regular speed	36
steady, to	*vt*	to stop something from moving around	34
steamer	*n*	a ship that uses steam power	9
steamship	*n*	a ship that uses steam power	12
strangle, to	*vi*	to be unable to breathe because you have something round your throat	35
strike, to	*vt*	to hit hard	31
stroll, to	*vi*	to walk in a relaxed way	28
struggle	*n*	a fight	44